MATCH WITS WITH

SHERLOCK HOLMES
Volume 2

MATCH WITS
WITH
SHERLOCK HOLMES

The Adventure of the Cardboard Box

A Scandal in Bohemia

adapted by
MURRAY SHAW
from the original stories by Sir Arthur Conan Doyle

illustrated by **GEORGE OVERLIE**

Carolrhoda Books, Inc./Minneapolis

To young mystery lovers everywhere

The author gratefully acknowledges permission granted
by Dame Jean Conan Doyle to use the Sherlock Holmes
characters and stories created by Sir Arthur Conan Doyle.

Library of Congress Cataloging-in-Publication Data

Shaw, Murray.
    Match wits with Sherlock Holmes. The Adventure of the Cardboard
Box. Scandal in Bohemia / adapted by Murray Shaw from the original
stories by Sir Arthur Conan Doyle : illustrated by George Overlie.
        p.   cm. — (Match wits with Sherlock Holmes : v. 2)
    Summary: Presents two adventures of Sherlock Holmes and Dr.
Watson, each accompanied by a section identifying the clues
mentioned in the story and explaining the reasoning used by Holmes
to put the clues together and come up with a solution. Also includes
a map highlighting the sites of the mysteries.
    ISBN 0-87614-386-9
    1. Children's stories. English. [1. Mystery and detective
stories. 2. Literary recreations.] I. Doyle. Arthur Conan. Sir,
1859-1920. II. Overlie, George, ill. III. Title. IV. Series:
Shaw, Murray, Match wits with Sherlock Holmes : v. 2.
PZ7.S53426Car   1990
[Fic]—dc20   89-22292
                                                    CIP
                                                     AC
Manufactured in the United States of America

1   2   3   4   5   6   7   8   9   10   99   98   97   96   95   94   93   92   91   90

CONTENTS

In the year 1887, Sir Arthur Conan Doyle created two characters who captured the imagination of mystery lovers around the world. They were Sherlock Holmes—the world's greatest fictional detective—and his devoted companion, Dr. John H. Watson. These characters have never grown old. For over a hundred years, they have delighted readers of all ages.

In the Sherlock Holmes stories, the time is always the late 1800s and the setting, Victorian England. Holmes and Watson live in London, on the second floor of 221 Baker Street. When Holmes travels through back alleys and down gaslit streets to solve crimes, Watson is often at his side. After Holmes's cases are complete, Watson records them. These are the stories of their adventures.

INTRODUCTION

Sherlock Holmes became a great detective because he observed the world carefully and made logical deductions from his observations. Watson recalls a discussion he had with Holmes about this process:

"Holmes, you have often spoken to me about observation and deduction," I said to him. "But surely one follows naturally from the other."

"Why, yes," Holmes replied, leaning back in his armchair and sending up thick blue wreaths of smoke from his pipe. "But many people fail to follow through to the point of deduction. For example, observation tells me that you visited the Wigmore Street Post Office this morning, but it is deduction that lets me know you sent off a telegram while you were there."

"You are right on both counts," I admitted. "But how did you know? I've told no one of my activities."

"It's more simple than you think, my dear Watson," said Holmes, chuckling at my surprise. "You have a bit of red clay sticking to the instep of your left boot. As far as I have seen, a clay of this type is found at only one place in our neighborhood—across from the post office, where they are building a new pavement. That much is observation. Now putting those facts together is deduction."

As always I was a little mystified by his powers. "And how did you deduce the telegram?"

He leaned forward and smiled. "I sat opposite you this morning as you worked on your books, yet I never saw you write a letter. Nor did I see you carrying anything as you left here. Furthermore, I noted that you already have a sheet of stamps and a bundle of postcards in your desk. Therefore, what reason would you have to go to the post office but to send a wire? One needs only to eliminate the improbable possibilities to find the truth."

"Indeed, Holmes," I said with admiration, "your techniques must be sound, for your solutions continue to be correct." And once again I saw clearly how carefully a mind must work if one wants to become a master of detection.

"*They had stopped rowing and were talking quietly when I reached them.*"

THE ADVENTURE OF THE CARDBOARD BOX

I t was a blazing day in August, and our rooms on Baker Street held the heat like an oven. I was sitting back, dreaming of an escape to the beaches of Brighton, and Holmes was lying back on the sofa reading. There was not a bead of sweat on his high forehead.

"Watson," he said, gesturing with newspaper in hand, "did you happen to read about the strange packet sent to a Miss Susan Cushing of Croydon?"

"No," I replied, "I must have overlooked it."

"It's really quite interesting. Here it is, after the financial column. Perhaps you could read it aloud." He handed me the paper and sat back, closing his eyes so he could concentrate.

I read the following report from the *Daily Chronicle:*

A GRUESOME PACKET

Miss Cushing, who lives at Cross Street in Croydon, is the victim of a cruel and senseless joke. That is, of course, unless something worse is being threatened.

At two o'clock yesterday afternoon, a small packet wrapped in brown paper was delivered to Miss Cushing by the regular post. Inside was a cardboard box filled with coarse sea salt. As she emptied the box, Miss Cushing was horrified to find two freshly cut human ears.

Miss Cushing is unaware of any reason for this mysterious occurrence. She is a maiden of fifty who has lived an uneventful, quiet life.

At one time, however, Miss Cushing rented rooms in her house to some medical students. Because they were loud and riotous, she had to ask them to leave. One of the students was from Belfast.

Now, the strange package had, in fact, been posted in Belfast, without a return address or note from the sender. Thus, police suspect that the contents of the package could be tokens taken from the dissecting room and sent to Miss Cushing by this medical student—a decidedly malicious way to revenge a grudge.

At present the case is being investigated by one of our top detective officers, Mr. Lestrade.

"Your friend Lestrade?" I asked, looking up.

"Precisely. He has written me a letter asking for help," said Holmes. "What do you say, Watson? Would you like to accompany us? It might be an intriguing case for your collection."

"I was looking for something to do to take my mind off the heat," I said with relief.

"Then kindly ring for a cab as I put on my boots."

——— ∽ ———

As we traveled southward on the train, a bit of rain fell, cooling the air. We stepped off the train at the Croydon platform and made our way past the High

Street to Cross Street. A neat row of two-story homes lined both sides of the street. Each had white stone steps, a short walk, and a black wrought-iron fence enclosing two feet of green.

Inspector Lestrade was standing outside Miss Cushing's address speaking to some white-aproned women with brooms from nearby stoops. Seeing us, Lestrade tipped his straw hat to the women and walked over to meet us. He looked as wiry and dapper as ever in a fresh linen suit.

"Good afternoon, Mr. Holmes, Dr. Watson," the young man greeted us. "I think this case will be to your liking because it's so unusual. At this point we have little to go on. The post office in Belfast was wired about the parcel, but no one remembers the person who sent it. Still, everything seems to lead back to the medical student."

"We shall see," said Holmes. "Shall we proceed?"

Lestrade tapped at the door. A young servant girl answered and brought us into a small front room. In a chair by the window, Miss Cushing sat embroidering. The brown curls on her forehead were streaked with gray and frizzled by the heat.

She looked up, and her gentle eyes seemed weary. "You'll find those dreadful things in the shed out back, Inspector," she said, "not in my home."

"Miss Cushing," said Lestrade, holding his hat in his hands, "I have only returned so my friend Mr. Holmes could take a look at the parcel and ask you a few questions."

Her meek face turned sour. "Why do you need to ask me more questions? I've told you I know nothing whatsoever about this. And I am not accustomed to all this commotion. I dislike having my name in the papers and police in my house."

Holmes stepped forward politely. "Miss Cushing, this has been annoying, indeed. We will disturb you as little as possible."

She sighed and motioned for us to make our way to the garden out back.

———— ✐ ————

Lestrade went into the small garden shed and came out carrying a yellow cardboard box, a piece of brown wrapping paper, and some string. We sat on the garden bench, and Holmes began examining the articles.

"This string is of stiffer stuff than is necessary for a parcel, and it carries a peculiar smell. What are your conclusions from this, Inspector?"

"It is a piece of tarred twine," said Lestrade, "like that used at sea."

"Exactly," said Holmes. "And instead of untying the knot, Miss Cushing cut the string. This leads one to look more closely at the knot itself. It is of a type used for trimming sails."

"A very neat sailor's knot," Lestrade agreed.

Holmes then picked up the wrapping paper. Lestrade and I watched him closely.

"The paper smells slightly of coffee, and the address is printed in black ink with large, uneven letters."

They read:

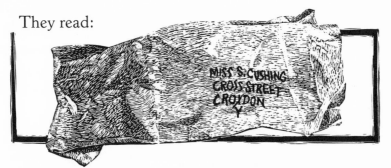

"The handwriting is masculine and uneducated. The man spelled Croydon with an *i*, but the post corrected it, making it a *y*. It would seem, then, that this man never actually lived in Croydon since he cannot spell it correctly."

"So far, so good," I said, enjoying the sight of Holmes at work.

"Now for the box," said Lestrade.

In his precise way, Holmes looked at the yellow box. "This box is the kind used for tobacco, and the salt in it is the kind used for preserving sealskins and wolf pelts."

On top of the large salt crystals were two ears of different sizes. One was small and fine, with a slight pink color. The other was larger and sunburned. Both were pierced for earrings.

"This is a strange practical joke," I murmured, sharing Miss Cushing's disgust.

"This is no joke," said Holmes. "Undoubtedly, this is murder."

Lestrade and I stared at Holmes in disbelief.

"But, Mr. Holmes," said Lestrade, "these could easily have been taken from the dissecting room by the medical student. There is no reason to suspect murder."

"Consider this," Holmes replied. "In a dissecting room, the ears would have been injected with a preserving fluid. These have been put in salt. In addition, Inspector, the ears were not cut with the smooth blade of a surgeon."

Lestrade still objected. "But what reason would there be to send poor Miss Cushing this evidence of so foul a crime? Unless she is the most clever actress in the world, she seems to know nothing about all of this—and better for her that she does not."

"That is the mystery we must solve," said Holmes. "But by this evidence, it seems there has been a double murder—a woman and a man. Also, the ears look like they have not been preserved for long. Therefore, we must presume the tragedy happened on Wednesday or Tuesday, since the package was posted on Thursday. Now why would the murderer want Miss Cushing to know that these crimes were committed?"

Holmes paused so the inspector and I could ponder the question. "The murderer," he explained, "would either send these ears to cheer Miss Cushing or to pain her. But if these were the reasons, why did she call the police? She wouldn't want the police to know that she was aware of the murders. No, if Miss Cushing had known about the murders, she could easily have buried the ears, and none would have been the wiser."

Holmes stood and turned toward the house. "Inspector, this is a tangle that needs unraveling. I would like to ask a few questions of Miss Cushing."

"Then I must ask you to excuse me," said Lestrade.

"Miss Cushing is quite tired of my questions already, and I have other things I must attend to. I will be at the police station if you need assistance." He departed, and we headed for the back door.

As we walked into the front room, we saw Miss Cushing staring absently out the window. The afternoon sun shone down on her, glinting off her fine loop earrings and the emerald ring on her right hand. Holmes paused in his step and stared at her profile. She turned when she sensed our presence.

"Mr. Holmes," she said sincerely, "now that you have seen those things, you can see why I am convinced a mistake has been made. I cannot think of anyone who would hate me so."

"You may be right, Miss Cushing." He was looking at something beyond her head, and he seemed both startled and excited. "You have two sisters, I believe?"

"Why, yes. How did you know?" she asked, peering at Holmes suspiciously.

"I observe the portrait on the mantle behind you," he replied. "One woman in it is undoubtedly yourself, and the other two look so much like you that I must assume you are all related."

"Yes, they are my younger sisters—Mary on the right and Sarah on the left," she said, pointing them out.

"And the photo on the piano looks like your sister Mary with a young ship steward," Holmes continued.

She smiled in a relieved way, glad to be on a comfortable topic. "Yes, that is Mary with her husband, Jim Browner. That was taken before they were married, when he was working on a South American shipping line. Once they married, he changed ships so he wouldn't have to leave Mary alone so much. He now works for a London-to-Ireland line."

"Ah, the *Conquerer*, perhaps?"

"No, it was the *May Day* last time I heard. Mary hasn't written for a while, so I'm not sure." She talked easily now, like a lonely person who has finally found an audience. She talked on about her sisters, her home, and the medical students that had caused her such trouble.

Holmes listened intently, asking a question here and there. "Since you and your sister Sarah are both unmarried, wouldn't it have worked out well for you to live together?"

"We did for a while, Mr. Holmes, but after a few months, Sarah left. She has quite a temper and can be terribly meddlesome. Sarah went to visit Mary and her husband in Liverpool, and when she returned, she got a house in Wallington on New Street."

"Did Sarah get on well with Mary and her husband?"

"Yes, they used to be such close friends, all three of them. When Sarah is in a good mood, she can make anyone laugh, and she could always tease Jim into loud laughter. But something went wrong during the last few months Sarah was there. Toward the end, Sarah couldn't write a word harsh enough for Jim Browner. I imagine she meddled in his life as well."

Holmes nodded with satisfaction and thanked her for her time. "I'm sure, Miss Cushing," he added in his soothing way, "that you have nothing to do with this affair."

— ∽ —

Leaving Miss Cushing's home, we hailed a cab. "Watson, we must strike while the iron is hot." I was unsure what he was talking about, but I followed his striding figure to the cab. We headed straightaway for the house of the other Miss Cushing. What, I thought, could Miss Sarah Cushing tell us about her sister's mysterious package?

The cab pulled up in front of a neat brick house, which looked much like the ones on Cross Street. Just as we arrived, a young doctor, with a black bag in hand and stethoscope swinging from his neck, left Miss Cushing's and started walking up the street. Holmes whistled sharply under his breath. "Something's up here," he murmured to himself. He told our driver to wait, and we approached the door.

A stately man in black answered our knock. "Miss Cushing is ill and cannot be disturbed," he said. "She has a sudden brain fever. The doctor expects that she shall be better in a few weeks, so you may call again at that time." He bowed and closed the door.

"In that case," said Holmes with a half smile, turning back to the cab, "we can wrap up this case. But first I need to send two telegrams—one to the *May Day* line and the other to the Liverpool police. Then we can meet Inspector Lestrade at the station."

"But Holmes," I protested, "what information do we have to go on? Nothing certain has been revealed."

"You shall see, my dear Watson, that everything is evident already. It needs only to be confirmed."

———— ✑ ————

As we headed to the train station, we stopped at a post office to send the telegrams and at a pub for a quick meal. By the time we arrived at the London police station, the sky had already taken on the warm glow of dusk.

Lestrade met us at the door with telegrams in hand.

Holmes tore them open eagerly. "Ha!" he said, "the crimes have been confirmed, Inspector. You can prepare to put the murderer behind bars."

Lestrade laughed. "Surely you must be joking."

"I certainly am not." Holmes looked insulted. "Here is the man's name, but you will not be able to take him into custody until tomorrow night at the earliest." He wrote something on the back of his calling card and handed it to the inspector.

"We shall return in two days,' said Holmes, "to hear the full story from the murderer himself. Until then." He tipped his hat to the bewildered Lestrade, and we left.

——— ∾ ———

After dinner Holmes settled back in his chair and filled his pipe. "Watson, are you prepared to write the conclusion of this case for your collection?"

"No, of course not, Holmes," I replied, exasperated. "Everything seems to be mere suspicion. I suppose that you think Jim Browner is the murderer. But we do not even yet know who has been killed or why the murderer would bother Miss Cushing."

Holmes shook his head with mock disappointment. "No, my dear Watson, let us begin again with an open mind. Early on in the investigation, we noticed that *Croydon* was misspelled on the package's address. Thus, it seems unlikely that the package was sent by a medical student who had once lived in the town. At the same time, we noted that the string, knot, and salt all pointed to someone from a ship. Therefore, we are able to deduce that the murderer is probably a seaman—such as Jim Browner."

I nodded, carefully noting his reasoning.

Holmes continued, "The parcel was addressed to a Miss S. Cushing, yet Miss Susan Cushing appeared in sincere confusion and unaware of any crime. However, Miss Cushing has two sisters. One sister, Miss Sarah Cushing, once lived at the same address as Miss Susan. And she also has the same first initial. This permits us to believe that the parcel was received by the wrong Miss S. Cushing."

"A fine piece of work, my dear Holmes, but who are the murder victims? And what makes you so sure Browner is their killer?" I asked in frustration.

"Did you notice what a fine and delicate ear Miss Cushing has?"

"No, but what has that to do with it?" Then it slowly dawned on me, and I gasped.

Holmes smiled grimly. "I doubt the story is pretty. One of the telegrams said Browner's ship made its last stop in Belfast. It should come to port in London tomorrow night. We had better wait to get the details from Browner himself."

———— ✍ ————

Two days later we met Lestrade at the police station.

"We have your man, Mr. Holmes," the inspector reported. "And it's a grisly story he has to tell."

Inspector Lestrade led us to a row of cells. In the last cell on the right sat a man with his head buried in his large, rough hands. He was moaning softly, rocking back and forth. A few day's growth of beard covered his narrow chin, and his eyes had the look of someone who could see nothing.

Holmes pulled up a chair from the corner of the cell and sat down so his eyes were level with those of the man. "Now, Mr. Browner," Holmes said in a soft voice, "why did you kill your wife and the other man?"

"It was all Sarah's fault," Browner wailed. "I loved

Mary, and Sarah would have none of it. She came to visit after she left Susan's, and Mary and I welcomed her. I thought all was well, but one day I came home earlier than expected. Mary was shopping, and when I asked Sarah where Mary was, she got angry. 'Can't you ever be content with my company, Jim?' she asked me. 'I'm in love with you,' she said. I was shocked. I put out my hand and said, 'Oh, Sarah, my lass, I'm so sorry.' She clutched my hand in both of hers, and they burned as if she were in a fever. I was afraid of her, and I pulled back my hand. Then she laughed in a strange, high-pitched way and left the room."

The man held his head, running a hand through his thick brown hair as he spoke. "That's when the trouble began. Her love turned to hate, and she

started telling lies about me to Mary. I lost my temper more and more often, and Mary started to distrust
me. I should have asked Sarah to leave, but Mary
wanted her to stay. Then Sarah started bringing a
sailor friend of hers over, Alec Fairbairn. The three
of them would go off together while I was at sea. I
grew more and more jealous. I told Sarah that if she
ever brought Fairbairn back into my house, I'd send
her one of his ears for a keepsake. She just laughed at
me in her devilish way, and a few days later she left."

Browner shook his head and said with despair, "I
thought things would improve, but they didn't. Soon
afterward I left the ship earlier than usual so I could
have a long talk with Mary. As I neared my house, a
cab passed me. Inside, my wife and Fairbairn were
sitting as cozy as two people can. I went out of my
head with anger and jealousy, and I hailed a cab to
follow them.

"They went straight to the train station. I mixed in
with the crowd at the platform and overheard them
ask for tickets to New Brighton. So I bought a ticket
and followed them there. When they arrived, they
headed for the lake to rent a boat. It was getting on
near evening, and a light haze was coming down over
the lake. They rowed their boat out into the middle of
it, never dreaming that I was following them."

As the man talked, his voice became more filled
with emotion. "It's all foggy in my head now, as foggy
as that lake. They had stopped rowing and were talking
quietly when I reached them. Mary saw me first and

screamed. Fairbairn tried to grab an oar, but I lunged at him, slamming an oar down onto his head. Mary moved to help him, and somehow she got hit too. Then it was as if I woke up, and they were both lying there dead. All I could think of was Sarah's mocking laugh. So I drew my knife and cut off their ears. I wanted Sarah to suffer for the evil she had caused."

He looked up at Holmes. "I killed them quick, and they are killing me slow. It matters not if you hang me; I shall be dead or mad before morning."

Holmes stood up as the man started once more to weep. Inspector Lestrade asked one of the police officers to bring a clergyman, and we left the cell.

Once outside the station, our eyes had to adjust to the sunlight. The London street was as busy as ever. Carriages were passing back and forth. Men with hats and canes, and women in loose belled skirts were walking swiftly in all directions. It was a relief after Browner's dark cell and tragic story. Holmes turned to me and said solemnly, "What is the meaning of it all, Watson? Reason falls short in explaining the wild passions of the heart. None of it makes sense to me."

I had no answer for him. The ways of love and hate are as mysterious to me as the cases he is able to solve.

Now that the full story has been told, the clues all make sense. Sherlock Holmes, though, knew most of the story before Browner told it. How did he know? Check the **CLUES** *to find out. With this case behind you, you'll be ready to join Holmes and Watson on their next adventure.*

CLUES
that led to the solution of
The Adventure of the
Cardboard Box

 When Holmes saw Miss Cushing's profile, he noticed that her ear was very much like the one he had seen in the box. Then he saw the picture of the sisters. Because of the striking resemblances among the three women, he felt certain that the ear in the box belonged to Mary or Sarah.

 The twine and salt from the box indicated someone familiar with the sea. When Holmes discovered that Miss Cushing had a brother-in-law who was a steward on an England-Ireland shipping line, Holmes suspected Browner was involved.

 Holmes often gets the information he needs by cleverly providing the wrong answers to his own questions. To discover the correct name of Browner's ship, the *May Day,* Holmes asked Miss Cushing if it were the *Conquerer.*

The story of Sarah's temper made Holmes suspect that she was also involved in the murders. To confirm that Sarah was not the sister murdered, Holmes went to visit her. He discovered that she was alive but very ill. He concluded, therefore, that Sarah had read the newspaper account and now knew who had been murdered and why. Her guilt and horror had made her critically ill.

Knowing Sarah was alive, Holmes deduced that Mary must be dead. To check this, he wired the Liverpool police to see if she were at home. They telegraphed back that there had been no answer at her house for the past three days. Holmes was sure then that Mary had been murdered.

Holmes could not conclude if Browner was the murderer or the man murdered. So Holmes wired the shipping line to find out whether or not Browner had reported for work and if the ship had stopped at Belfast. When the shipping company telegraphed back that Browner was at work and that the ship had stopped at Belfast on Thursday, Holmes knew Browner was the murderer.

One mystery still remained: Who was the man killed? Holmes suspected the man was a sailor because his ear was sunburned and pierced for an earring. But only Browner and Sarah knew the man's name and exactly why he had been killed.

"As she stepped into the carriage, I saw her face."

A SCANDAL IN BOHEMIA

It was a cool March night in 1888, and the gas lamps threw clear streams of light onto the cobblestone pavements and brick houses of Baker Street. I had not seen much of Holmes recently because I had married and set up household with my new bride some distance away. On this particular evening, I was returning home by way of Baker Street after seeing a patient. When I looked up at my former lodgings, I saw Holmes's silhouette in the window of the second-story sitting room. He was pacing, as he often did when deep in thought, his shoulders thrown forward and his pipe in his mouth.

Seeing there was excitement afoot, I decided to look in on Holmes. As I took the stairs and stepped into the room, Holmes stopped his pacing and looked at me with delight. "Ah, Watson, come in. You're looking well. And you've arrived at the perfect time. An interesting note came to me in the latest post. Here, you may read it."

He tossed me a piece of expensive, heavy paper with a rose tint. The letter had no date, signature, or return address. I read the letter aloud.

This evening, at precisely fifteen to eight, a
gentleman shall call on you to discuss a matter
of the deepest regard. You have been chosen
because of the fine service you have given to the
Royal Houses of Europe. It is with great trust
that you are being contacted. Please be in your
chambers at this hour, and do not be disturbed
if your visitor remains masked.

"This is indeed a note of strange consequence. What do you suppose it means, Holmes?" I asked.

"I have no data yet, my dear Watson, and I do not propose theories without that," said Holmes. "First let us examine the note. Does it lead you to any conclusions?"

I turned the paper over in my hands and put it up to the light, trying to imitate my friend's methods. "It's a high-class paper with a strange watermark that is not a familiar trademark. I would say it is foreign."

"Precisely," said Holmes, happy with my progress as a detective. "It's a kind of paper made in the German-speaking country of Bohemia. I would suspect our caller to be a member of that country's ruling class. But we shall see. It is a quarter to eight now, and I hear someone on the street."

We went to the windows and looked down to see an elaborate carriage and two beautiful chestnut horses stopped on the street below us.

"Well, Watson," said Holmes, "at the very least, there is money involved in this case."

A moment later there was a knock at the door.

"Come in," bid Holmes, and a powerfully built man strode in. Hatless, he stood six feet six, his back unusually straight. A black mask covered his eyes above a long handlebar mustache and a heavy jaw. He carried a gold-headed cane and had a royal blue cape.

"My note came to you?" he asked. His strong German accent made him difficult to understand.

"Yes, it did," said Holmes, walking to meet him. "Please be seated. This is my trusted friend Dr. Watson. You may speak as freely with him as with me."

The gentleman nodded crisply and took a seat in the chair next to the fireplace. "You may address me as Count Von Kramm," he said in a commanding voice. "You must treat this visit with the utmost secrecy. No mention must be made of this matter for at least two years. Do I have your sworn promises?"

"You do," we agreed.

"Please excuse the mask, gentlemen. I am in the service of a man who demands that I do not reveal my identity or his."

"I deduced as much," said Holmes dryly.

"My reason for calling on you is to prevent a scandal to the great House of Ormstein, the famous royal family of Bohemia."

"I'm also aware of that," Holmes said, lounging back in his armchair and closing his eyes. After a moment Holmes opened his eyes and said, "Your Majesty, I know well that you are Wilhelm Von Ormstein, King of Bohemia. I could advise you better if you would state your case openly."

The man sprang out of his chair and began to pace. Then he turned to face Holmes, tearing his mask from his face. "Yes, you are correct! I *am* the king. This matter is so delicate I could not trust it to another. I can see you are truly the master they say you are."

"The facts, Your Highness?"

The king sat down once more. "About five years ago, while in Warsaw, I met a well-known opera singer. Is the name Irene Adler familiar to you?"

Holmes looked over at me, sitting next to his files. "Kindly look her up in my index, will you, Watson?"

Holmes kept a fact file of important people, places, and things mentioned in the daily newspapers. I read:

Born in Liverpool—1858; contralto; sang at
La Scala in Milan, Italy; Prima Donna of Imperial
Opera of Warsaw; left stage; living in London.

"Very well," said Holmes. "I imagine that you became involved with this woman, and now there are some items given to her that you would like returned."

"Yes," said the king, looking boldly at Holmes. "They are letters of a private nature, and it is quite necessary that I have them back."

"Was there a secret marriage?"

"No."

"Any legal papers?"

"None."

"Then, Your Majesty, it seems you are quite safe. Miss Adler cannot blackmail you with your personal letters, because they can easily be forged."

"But they were written on my private paper, with my seal."

"They can be duplicated."

"My photograph?"

"It can be bought."

"But we are in it together."

"Ah," said Holmes, "then you are correct. This photograph must be recovered."

"Yes. I've tried to buy it from her, but she laughed at me. Twice burglars in my pay have broken into her house, but nothing was found. Once we had her luggage taken when she traveled." He paused and added, "Irene is as clever as she is beautiful."

"What does she intend to do with the photograph?"

"She wants to ruin me rather than have me marry anyone else. I recently became engaged to Clothilde Lothman Von Saxe-Meningen, the second daughter of the King of Scandinavia. Miss Adler threatened to send the photo and the letters to my fiancée. This would end our engagement and endanger the relations between my country and that of the princess."

"How do you know Miss Adler has not done this already?" Holmes asked.

"She is a woman of strong will but one who keeps her word," the king answered. "She swore that she would send these items to my intended bride on the exact day the betrothal is announced. And she will keep her word precisely. The announcement is due on Monday."

"Ah," said Holmes, yawning casually. "We have three days yet. You'll be staying in London until then, will you not?"

The king stood up, and his large frame made the room seem small. "I'll be staying at the Langham Hotel under the name of Count Von Kramm. You have complete freedom to do as you see fit." Opening his purse, the king withdrew a considerable sum of money—seven hundred pounds in notes and three hundred in gold coins.

Holmes took the money and went to his desk to write him a receipt.

"If more is needed," added the king, "I will provide it. This is a matter of great importance, or I would not take such measures. Miss Adler can be found at Briony Lodge on Serpentine Avenue, in the St. John Wood's area."

Holmes nodded but did not seem overly concerned. "One other question, Your Majesty. Was the picture built into a frame?"

"Yes, a large and very ornate one."

"Precisely what I had hoped. Then I trust we shall have good news for you soon."

With long strides, the king left the room.

"Watson," Holmes said, "I could use your assistance in this case. Would you be so kind as to return tomorrow at three o'clock?"

"Certainly," I said, excited at the prospect of once more joining Holmes on one of his investigations.

I returned to the Baker Street lodgings promptly at three, but Holmes was not there. Unsure of his whereabouts, I decided to wait. At about four o'clock, I heard someone stumbling on the steps. Then in stepped a drunken-looking groom with stained trousers and shirt. Though I was accustomed to my friend's amazing disguises, I had to look three times before I was certain it was Holmes. Without a word, he retreated into his bedroom and returned in a respectable tweed suit, looking like his usual self. He stretched himself out by the fire and began to laugh.

"Watson, you'll never imagine what I have been doing this afternoon."

"It's probable," I said, "that you were spying on Miss Adler's house."

"Quite correct, but the result was most uncommon." Holmes was flushed with excitement, like a man describing a heated race. "While I was helping some grooms in the neighborhood with their horses, I gained a wealth of information. Miss Adler has turned the head of every man in the area. From their report, she is the daintiest thing under a bonnet on this planet. She lives quietly, sings at concerts, and drives out each day at five to return exactly at seven. She has only one visitor—Mr. Godfrey Norton—a handsome attorney who calls twice a day. No one is sure if Mr. Norton is Miss Adler's attorney, beau, or friend."

Holmes raised an eyebrow. "I thought it best to observe all this myself, so I ambled down the street to Briony Lodge. The house resembles a French villa.

It has a garden out back, and the front rooms are built right up to the avenue. The parlor has full-length windows that reach almost to the ground and are shut with simple fasteners.

"Just as I had finished examining the lodge," said Holmes, "a hansom cab drove up, and out jumped a dark, elegant gentleman. He signaled for the cabby to wait and rushed to the door. Through the window I could see the gentleman walking back and forth excitedly. He was moving his hands in the air as if he were making a point to someone. Then he turned and came out of the house a moment later. Checking his watch, he hurried to the cab and told the cabby to drive like the devil to the Church of St. Monica on Edgware Road. He had to be there in twenty minutes sharp.

"I was wondering what I should do when a fancy little carriage drove up. The woman in question, Miss Adler, shot out of the house. As she stepped into the carriage, I saw her face. It was one a man might die for!"

Holmes's last sentence and excited voice were certainly unexpected. Never before had his cool-headed reasoning allowed him to comment on a woman's charms. From this I deduced that Irene Adler must indeed be an exceptional woman.

Holmes continued telling his story at a rapid pace. "Miss Adler cried out to the coachman, 'The Church of St. Monica, and half a sovereign if you arrive in twenty minutes!' Why, Watson, this was too good a game to lose. I jumped into a passing cab and yelled to the cabby the same half-sovereign offer. With sweat rolling off the horses, we arrived at the church door a few minutes behind the others. The church was empty except for a small threesome at the altar—a clergyman, Miss Adler, and Mr. Norton. I slipped in quietly, trying to look like a parishioner. Suddenly, to my surprise, the three turned and faced me. Mr. Norton came running up and seized my hand.

"'Thank God,' he cried. 'You are just in time to be a witness and make this marriage legal!'

"Before I knew it, I was mumbling responses they whispered in my ear. Then they were all thanking me, and the lovely bride gave me a sovereign. And, my dear Watson, I do believe I will wear it on my watch chain from now on as a souvenir of this extraordinary occasion."

Holmes displayed his golden coin with pride.

"This *is* unusual," I said. "What happened next?"

Holmes, regaining his calm manner, resumed his story. "At this point I was concerned that they might leave the country and the photograph would remain missing. But as the new bride parted from her husband, she told him that she would drive out in the park at five as usual. So I came back here as swiftly as possible to make arrangements."

"And they are?" I asked.

Holmes stood up and faced me. "Watson," he said seriously, "I need your cooperation. You don't mind breaking the law, do you?"

"Not if it's for a good cause."

"Oh, the cause is a good one and certainly worth it."

"Then I'm your man, Holmes. What am I to do?" I was happy to once again feel the familiar thrill of the chase.

"It's nearly five," said Holmes, striding around the room, picking up various items and putting them in his pockets. "In two hours Miss Adler, or rather Mrs. Norton, will be coming back from her drive in the park. We must be at Briony Lodge to meet her. Leave the rest to me."

Then he paused. "However," he cautioned, "I insist on one point. You must not interfere with anything, come what may. Is that clear? It is most important."

"Am I to be neutral?"

"Positively. Do nothing whatsoever. There will be some unpleasantness. But do not join in or try to stop it. It will end by me being carried into her house. A few minutes later, the sitting room window will open. You are to be close to that window, watching me. I will be visible. When I raise my hand, you are to throw this plumber's smoke rocket into the room." He handed me a long, hard roll, which was shaped like a cigar, from out of his pocket.

"It will light by itself when it hits the ground," he continued. "When you see a wisp of smoke, cry out 'Fire,' and others will join you. Then make your way to the street corner, where I will meet you."

"You may rely on me, Holmes," I assured him. His plan sounded peculiar, but I had no doubts that if I knew everything, it would seem entirely reasonable.

Holmes went into his bedroom and soon returned, looking like a gentle, simple-minded country clergyman. A broadcloth hat, baggy trousers, white tie, and worn black coat had transformed the Holmes I knew. He peered at me through small wire spectacles and piously folded his hands. I had to laugh. The stage had lost a fine actor when Holmes turned his talents to solving crime.

——— ∽ ———

At ten minutes to seven, we were out on Serpentine Avenue, in front of Briony Lodge. Dusk was laying a rosy tinge on the air as the gas lamps were being lit.

There were more people about than I would have
expected. A group of shabbily dressed men were
laughing together under one of the lamps, and a scissors
grinder was pushing his cart up the street. Near the
gate, two guardsmen were flirting with a maid, and a
few others were milling around farther down the lane.

Holmes was filled with nervous energy, pacing to
and fro in front of the house. "Now, Watson, where do
you expect she has hidden the photo?" he asked. "It's
too large for her to carry with her. She could have
given it to her banker, but I think not. She is deter-
mined to use it in a few days. And this is really too
delicate a matter for a banker. It must be in her house."

"But it has been burglarized twice," I protested.

"Ah, but they did not know where to look. I'm
going to have the woman show me where it is."

"But how, Holmes? She will refuse."

Holmes smiled secretly. "She may not be able to,
Watson. We shall see."

Just then a carriage approached the lodge.

"Now for my part," Holmes said, leaving me to start
strolling past the lodge's drive.

As the carriage slowed, several guardsmen rushed
to open door for the woman inside, in hopes of earning
a coin or two. One shoved another, and a fierce quarrel
broke out. In an instant the lady was in the midst of a
group of angry men. Holmes dashed forward to protect
her, but just as he reached her, he gave a cry and fell to
the ground with blood flowing freely from his face.
At that the men all took to their heels, while some

onlookers moved in to help the fallen man.

"He's badly injured," one woman cried. Her companion, a man, agreed and said to Miss Adler, "We can't leave him lying in the street. May we bring him into your house?"

"Yes," Miss Adler said. "Please bring him into the sitting room and lay him on the sofa."

Slowly and carefully, two men carried Holmes into her parlor and placed him on her couch. I observed everything from my place by the window.

As I watched this beautiful woman act so generously, I felt heartily ashamed of the part I was playing in Holmes's scheme. Then Holmes suddenly seemed to revive and raised his hand to motion for air. The maid threw open the window near me and went back to attend to Holmes. True to my word, I tossed in the smoke bomb. A dark cloud began to fill the room, and I yelled, "FIRE" at the top of my voice. All the people on the street took up the same cry.

Inside, people were rushing around until the maid found the bomb and yelled out "false alarm." I slipped away to the street corner, where I was soon joined by the disguised Holmes. We walked swiftly down Serpentine Avenue without talking until we reached the quieter streets of Edgware Road.

"You did well, Watson. It couldn't have gone better."

"So you have the photograph?" I asked.

"No. But she showed me where it is. All that remains is to retrieve it."

"I'm still in the dark. How did you manage it?"

"As you probably supposed, all those people were in my employ and followed my directions. When the fight broke out, I had a little red theater paint in my palm. I clapped my hand to my forehead and fell to the ground. Since I looked quite pitiful, Miss Adler had little choice but to care for my needs. It's a trick that often works."

"I had figured as much."

"Once the cry of 'Fire' went up, she ran straight to a sliding panel just above the bellpull. Within seconds she had a frame partly pulled out. Then she heard the maid call out that it was a false alarm, and she quickly replaced it. Turning, she saw the rocket on the carpet and ran from the room. I would have taken the photograph at the time, but her coachman came in and seemed to be watching me. So I decided it was safer to act as if I had recovered from my injuries and leave immediately. I did not want to rush things and possibly lose all."

"But what now?"

"I'll call the king and arrange for the three of us to go to her house early tomorrow morning. We shall be shown into her sitting room to wait for her. Before she has the chance to see who has called, we'll have the photograph and be gone."

By this time we had reached our doorstep on Baker Street. As Holmes looked for his key, someone passing said, "Goodnight, Mr. Sherlock Holmes."

We turned to see who spoke, but many people were on the street. The voice seemed to have come from a slim youth in a loose overcoat and bowler, who had continued on his way.

Holmes stopped, thinking he could place the voice. But he couldn't, so we went in.

—— ⌘ ——

Early the next morning, Holmes, the king, and I met at the gate of Briony Lodge.

"Do you have the photograph?" the king asked Holmes with eager anticipation.

"No, but we will soon," said Holmes. "You should know, though, that Irene Adler is married."

"Married?" said the king, startled. "But she cannot love the man."

"It is my hope that she does," said Holmes.

"But why?"

"Then she will bother you no further."

The king slumped a little, disappointed. "Yes, that is true. But it is a true pity that a woman such as Irene was not born a princess. What a Queen she would have become!"

Just then Miss Adler's elderly housekeeper came out of the door onto the stoop.

"Mr. Holmes?" she called out, looking from one of us to the next.

"Yes. I am Mr. Holmes," he said, surprised that she knew his name.

"My mistress told me that you would come to call," the woman said. "She left with her husband for the continent on the 5:15 a.m. train from the Charing Cross station."

"What!" Holmes staggered back a step, white with shock.

"Then the papers and photograph are also gone," the king moaned hoarsely.

"We shall see," said Holmes. He rushed past the housekeeper with us close behind him. The house was in wild disarray, with drawers open and cartons on the floor. Holmes ran to the bellpull, plunged his hand into the cabinet, and pulled out a photograph and letter. The picture was of Irene Adler in an evening gown. The letter was addressed:

Mr. Sherlock Holmes, Esquire
to be called for

My friend tore open the letter and read it aloud:

My dear Mr. Holmes,
  You took me in completely. Until after the alarm, I had no suspicions. But when I realized how I had betrayed myself, I began to think. A few months ago I had been warned that the king was planning to hire a detective. I knew that you were the best and most logical choice, if all I had heard of you were true. (Obviously, it is.) So at the time I did a little research and located your address.
  After the false alarm, I had my coachman watch you. Then I donned my own disguise and followed you to your door. At that point I could not resist wishing you goodnight. I knew for certain it was you when you turned to see who had called your name.
  From Baker Street I went straight to my husband's address. We decided it was best to leave England, so we will not be bothered further. Thus, you will find the nest empty.
  Tell your client to rest easy. I love and am loved by a better man than he. I will keep the photograph he is looking for as protection against

*him. But you have my word that I will not use
it for any other purpose. I leave this photograph
for him as a sign of my good faith.*
 I remain, my dear Holmes,
   Very truly yours,
   Irene Norton, née Adler

"What a woman!" cried the king. "What a shame she was not on my level."

Holmes looked at him coldly. "Indeed, she seems of another level entirely."

"As for your services, Mr. Holmes," said the king, "please take this emerald ring." He began to pull one of the many rings from his fingers when Holmes stopped him.

"Your Majesty, there is something I would value more highly."

"Name it."

"This photograph," said Holmes sincerely.

"Irene's photograph," the king cried in surprise. He hesitated and then said with a tinge of sadness, "Certainly, if that is what you wish." And he handed it to Holmes.

"Thank you, Your Majesty. I believe there is nothing more to be done." Then, without the shaking of a hand, Holmes turned away and headed straight back to Baker Street.

From that point on, Holmes never again referred to Irene Norton (née Adler) by her name. She has always been called, with the greatest honor—*the woman.* There has been no other for Holmes. She did what few could do—she outsmarted him.

Using his skills of disguise, Holmes was able observe the lovely Miss Adler from afar. Then he used clues about her character and human nature in general to form a plan that would make the woman reveal her hiding place. Thus, he helped prevent a crime from being committed. Go on to the **CLUES** *to see if you followed all the twists and turns in Holmes's reasoning.*

CLUES
that led to the solution of
A Scandal in Bohemia

 Since Miss Adler knew people were looking for her photograph and letters, Holmes reasoned that she would hide them in a place where she could watch them and get ahold of them easily. The most likely room in the house, therefore, was the front sitting room.

 Miss Adler was known to be a strong-willed woman, but one with a warm heart. Since burglary had failed, Holmes figured it would be better to appeal to the woman's kindness. So he created the character of the clergyman and the fight so Miss Adler would bring the injured Holmes into her house.

 In the case of a fire, most people try to save their most valued possessions before fleeing the building. By faking a fire, Holmes was able to force Miss Adler into revealing her hiding place.

 However, Holmes had made one mistake. He underestimated his opponent's awareness and intelligence. Because of Irene Adler's great respect for Holmes's capabilities, she suspected the fake fire was the work of the master detective. She, therefore, used her acting abilities and a disguise of her own to confirm her suspicions. Thus, Miss Adler became one of the few people ever to outsmart Sherlock Holmes.